Santa Mouse
Story and Songs

Follow along with
the story of Santa Mouse and
sing along when you see the
songs in red!

Santa Mouse
Story and Songs

Story and Songs by Michael Brown

Illustrated by Elfrieda DeWitt

BARNES
&NOBLE
BOOKS
NEW YORK

Who's the little friend on Santa's shoulder?
Santa Mouse!
Who is it we look for when it's colder?
Santa Mouse!

He's the one who once was just
A mouse without a name
Till he did a deed so very kind
When Christmas came.

Oh, who's the one who thought about
 a gift for
          Santa Claus?
Who's the one who wrapped a piece of
   cheese up
          With his paws?

Who's the little fellow with the biggest
   heart in all the house
          And with the whiskers?
Is it any wonder Santa named him
          Santa Mouse?

Once there was a little mouse

Who didn't have a name.

He lived in a great big house, this mouse,
The only mouse in the whole, wide house.

He used to play a game.

He'd daydream
  he had playmates

Who were friendly
  as could be.

While some of them
  would bring their dolls

And dress up
  and have tea,

There were others
who'd play cowboys

Or be Eskimos

Or Spanish.

But when he'd try
to touch them,

Like a bubble,
they would vanish.

Now, through the year,
this little mouse

Had saved one
special thing:

A piece of cheese!

The kind that makes an angel want to sing.

On Christmas Eve, he brushed his teeth,

And as he washed his paws,

He thought, "My goodness, no one gives
A gift to Santa Claus!"

He ran to get his pretty cheese,

Hurry up, hurry up,
Find the cheese,
Really got to find that cheese!
But how?

Hurry up, hurry up,
Find the cheese,
Hey,
There it is now!

And after he had found it,

The paper from some chewing gum
He quickly wrapped around it.

And then he climbed in bed and dreamed

That he was lifted high.

He woke to find that he was looking
Right in Santa's eye!

Santa Claus, Santa Claus,
He was looking at Santa Claus,
The one that ev'ryone loves because
He's Santa Claus.

"I thank you for my gift,"
said Santa.

"Tell me, what's your name?"

"I haven't any,"
said the mouse.

"You haven't?
That's a shame!

You know, I need a helper
As I travel house to house,
And I shall give a name to you:

I'll call you Santa Mouse."

Santa Mouse,
Santa Mouse,
You'll be leaving
your lonely house.

"So here's your beard,

and here's your suit,

And here's each shiny,

tiny

boot.

You mustn't sneeze, and don't you cough.
Just put them on, and we'll be off!"

Dasher and Dancer
Are hitched to the sleigh,
Suddenly it's Christmas,
What a happy day!

Comet and Prancer
Are eager to say
Suddenly it's Christmas,
Santa's on his way!

Then over all the rooftops,
On a journey with no end,
Away they went together,
Santa with his tiny friend.

Donder and Blitzen
will tell you it's true
Santa Claus is coming,
Someone else is too!

And so, this Christmas,
if you please,
Beneath the tree that's
in your house,
Why don't you leave
a piece of cheese?

You know
who'll thank you?

Santa Mouse!

Once there was a little mouse
Who lived all alone in a great, big house
With playmates who were all imaginary

Until one night St. Nick appeared,
Gave him a suit, hooked on a beard,
And took him on a trip so light and airy.

Who's the little friend on Santa's shoulder?
Santa Mouse!
Who is it we look for when it's colder?
Santa Mouse!

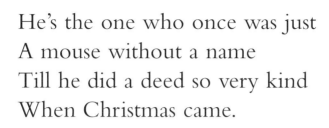

He's the one who once was just
A mouse without a name
Till he did a deed so very kind
When Christmas came.

Oh, who's the one who thought about a
gift for
Santa Claus?
Who's the one who wrapped a piece of
cheese up
With his paws?

Who's the little fellow with the biggest heart
in all the house
And with the whiskers?
Is it any wonder Santa named him
Santa Mouse?

Dasher and Dancer
Are hitched to the sleigh,
Suddenly it's Christmas,
What a happy day!

Comet and Prancer
Are eager to say
Suddenly it's Christmas,
Santa's on his way!

Vixen is jingling,
And Cupid is tingling,
They're all set to go,
And they know what to do.

Donder and Blitzen
Will tell you it's true
Suddenly it's Christmas,
What a merry Christmas,
Santa Claus is coming,
And Santa Mouse is coming, too!